A Christmas Mystery in Paris

CalmerTherapy

A very special mention to the staff and children for producing this book.

Alice Appleton   Lucy Ball   Cody Fairhurst
Alex Frizelle   Jacob Millen   Ruby Norwood
Leo Shepherd   Joshua Swan   Rosie Yates

Paul Blackburn   Nicola Wood

This book is dedicated to Claire Wealleans
and her boys Lee, Ben and Zac.

To her boys,
All your friends here at Calmer Therapy,
have written this book to
remember your incredible mum.
We hope this book is as special as she was
and it gives back just as much as she did,

Claire, a very special friend at Calmer Therapy,
sadly died this year.
Her dedication to raising awareness of cancer
was incredible and saved lives.
She was also an amazing mum to her boys,
Ben and Zac, who both have additional needs.
Claire helped make our wider community a more
accessible and inclusive place to be.
She devoted her life to helping make the world an
equal and safe environment for our children
to grow and thrive in.

First published in 2022 by Calmer Therapy Limited.
Registered Address: 19 Forster Avenue, Bedlington,
Northumberland, NE22 6EW
Registered Company Number: 10500366
Text and Illustrations Copyright © 2022 by Calmer Therapy Limited.
A CIP catalogue record for this book is available from the British Library

CalmerTherapy

ISBN: 978-1-8035236-5-1
Printed in United Kingdom
www.calmertherapy.org

Santa was delivering presents
to the children of Paris
when disaster struck!

His sleigh clipped the
top of the Eiffel Tower
and went spiraling into
the city below.

Back at North Pole HQ,
the 'Santa Lost' alarm began to blare.

Lacey and Alia, the elf twins jumped
in surprise.
They ran to their father, David.

" Dad, Dad! Santa's lost!"
" Dont be silly children,
Santa's never lost."
" But the alarm's going off."
"Oh Oh!" said David.

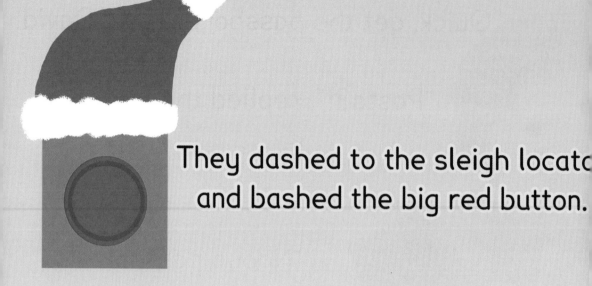

They dashed to the sleigh locato
and bashed the big red button.

"Last seen in Paris, France"
an electronic voice spoke in return.

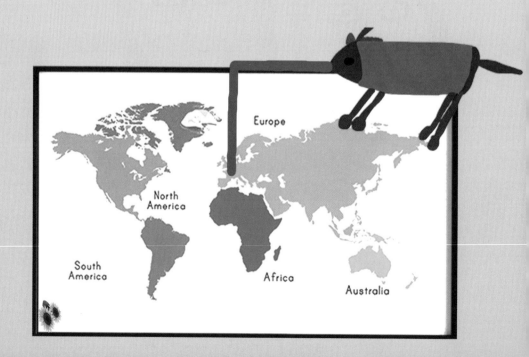

"Quick, get the passports," said David.

"Pasta?!", replied the twins.

"Noooo passports!
You silly elves!"

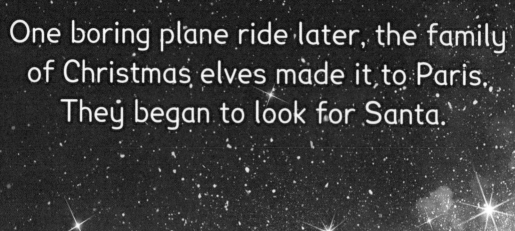

One boring plane ride later, the family
of Christmas elves made it to Paris.
They began to look for Santa.

They asked an ice cream man
if he had seen Santa.

The ice cream man hadn't,
but he had a delicious cone
of ice cream, so they had a rest
and shared that.

They asked a guard at the Eiffel Tower;
he hadn't seen Santa either.
He had been busy decorating
the Eiffel Tower and had fallen
into a box of decorations.
He now had tinsel on his head.

While the elves looked for Santa.
Ja'maka, the pure evil elf
followed them secretly.

She had revenge on her mind.

Ja'maka had never forgiven Santa for putting her on the naughty list.

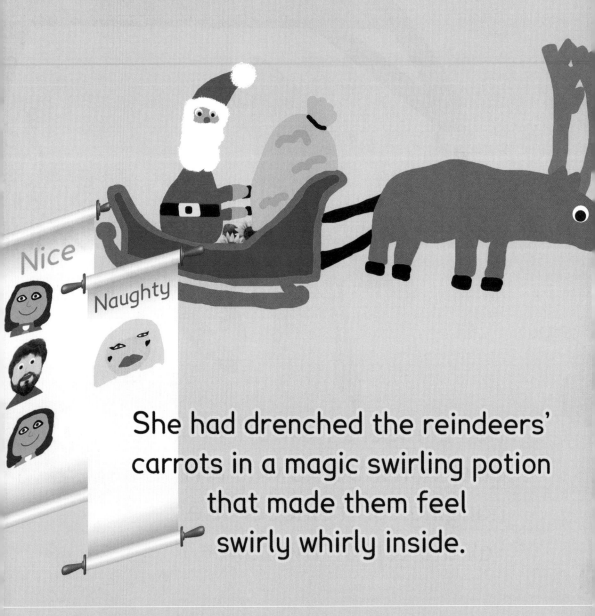

Nice

Naughty

She had drenched the reindeers' carrots in a magic swirling potion that made them feel swirly whirly inside.

That is why they hit the Eiffel Tower.

The reindeers flew off in all
directions. Santa was left
hanging for 'reindeer life'
at the top of the tower.

Not that the elves knew that yet.

Just as the elves were giving
up hope of ever finding Santa,
they looked near the Arc de Triomphe.
Would Santa be there?

No! Santa wasn't there.
But who is that?
A cactus in Paris.
" Have you seen Santa?"

"Bonjour! Hello!
Santa's not here I'm afraid.
Just me a cactus,
a spiky, sharp summer cactus!
Have you tried the Louvre?"

When they got to the Louvre,
they went over and looked for Santa.

No! Santa wasn't there.
But who is that?
A snowman is Paris.
"Have you seen Santa?"

Bonjour! Hello!
Santa's not here I'm afraid
Just me Melly, an immortal snowman!
Have you tried the Moulin Rouge?"

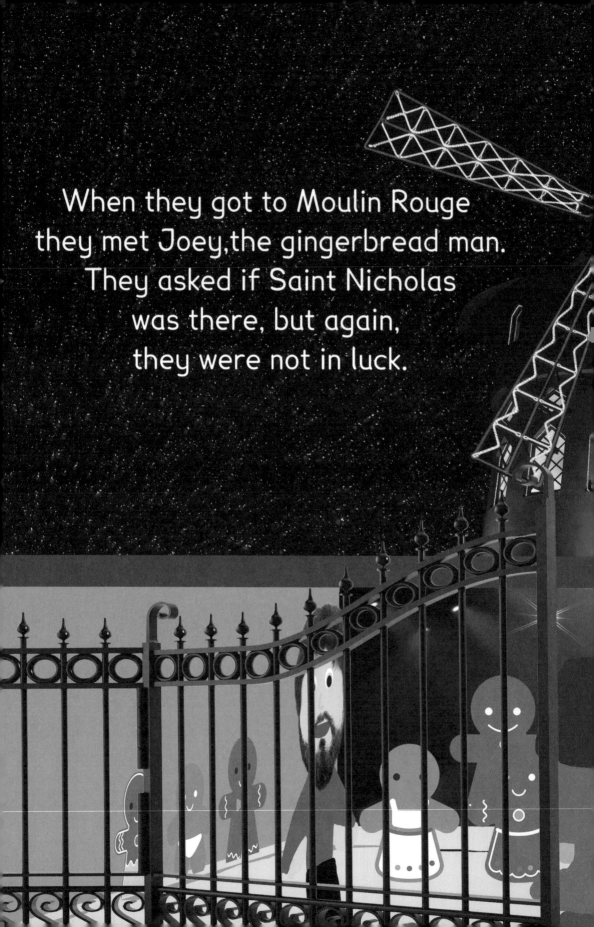

When they got to Moulin Rouge
they met Joey, the gingerbread man.
They asked if Saint Nicholas
was there, but again,
they were not in luck.

Joey was nervous,
"Have you tried the Versailles Palace?"

When the go there, they went in
and saw a tree dancing.
They walked towards him
and asked if he'd see Mr Claus.

"Bonjour! Hello!
Santa's not here I'm afraid.
Just me Salamander,
the Christmas tree!
Have you tried the
Eiffel Tower?"

"No, we'll try there."

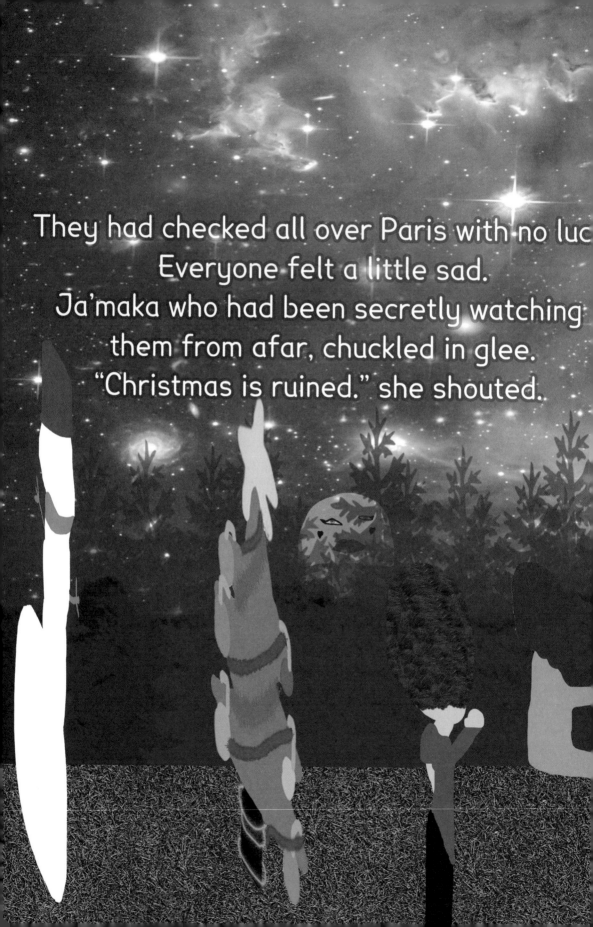

They had checked all over Paris with no luc
Everyone felt a little sad.
Ja'maka who had been secretly watching
them from afar, chuckled in glee.
"Christmas is ruined." she shouted.

Suddenly, a bright light blinded
the three elves,
the snowman,
the cactus,
the gingerbread man
and the Christmas tree.

They all looked up into the sky.
They couldn't believe their eyes.
In the sky was an angel.
The most beautiful angel
they had ever seen.

The angel's halo glowed brighter
and began to levitate away.
"Follow the halo, Follow the halo."
sang the angel.

They watched as the angel flew
through the air,
coming to a stop over the
Eiffel Tower.

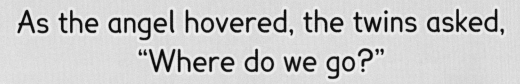

As the angel hovered, the twins asked,
"Where do we go?"

The angel pointed in the
    direction of the Eiffel Tower.
Her halo shone brightly
                above a red shape.
A big red shape.
            David cried out,
        " I know that big red shape.
            Thankyou angel,
            what do we call you?"

"Call me Claire," she replied.

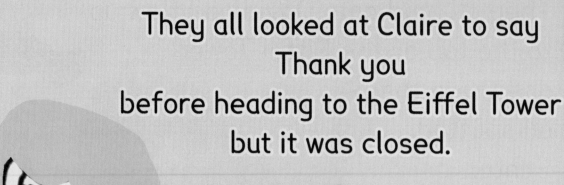

They all looked at Claire to say
Thank you
before heading to the Eiffel Tower
but it was closed.

Everyone became upset until
David told them a secret.

Amazingly he could fly!
They all held onto David and flew up
to the top of the Eiffel Tower
and there they
all spotted
Santa.

They all helped Santa down.

"Thank you for saving me,"
said a relieved Santa.
"But my sleigh is broken, and my reindeers
are scattered all over the world."

We can help!" said the Christmas friends.

Kevin the Christmas cactus filled
holes in the sleigh with his spikes.
Melly the snowman cooled down
the engine with his snowballs.

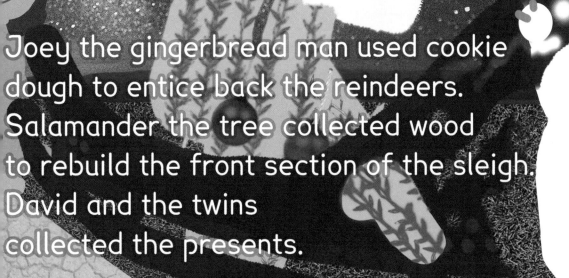

Joey the gingerbread man used cookie
dough to entice back the reindeers.
Salamander the tree collected wood
to rebuild the front section of the sleigh.
David and the twins
collected the presents.

With everything fixed, there was only
  one thing left for
Santa to do.

Claire the angel appeared,
 "Ah Claire my favourite angel",
                    said Santa.
"All I need now is your Christmas spirit."

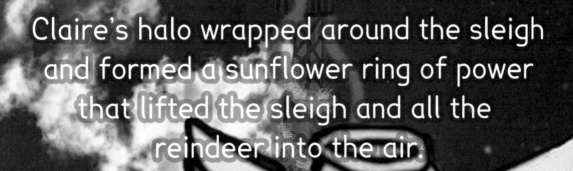

Claire's halo wrapped around the sleigh and formed a sunflower ring of power that lifted the sleigh and all the reindeer into the air.

The Christmas friends watched together as Santa flew alway to finish his deliveries.

Can you find the

sunflowers on each page?